GOODBYE WINTER, HELLO SPRING

KENARD PAK

Henry Holt and Company

New York

Hello, winter night.

Hello, snow.

Hello. From high up in the sky,

I drift down, down, down,

down, down,

down.

I fall through the sycamore branches.

I fall onto a husky's bushy tail.

Hello, frozen pond.

Hello, sleeping fish.

Hello. We huddle for a winter's sleep.

Over our frozen ceiling,

the wind sweeps away snowy dust.

Hello, glass house.

The swaying trees through my glass panels are like tall, slender ghosts.
The last logs are draped with snow.

Hello, winter brook.

Hello. Rocks and sticks are frozen
in the ice along my curving banks.

Hello, footprints in the snow.
Hello. We disappear as the snow covers us.

Hello, trees.
Hello. Our thin arms shudder
and lash in the rising
snowstorm.

Hello, empty nest.
Hello. Against the striking winds,
my twigs stay together!

Hello, winter storm.

Good morning, orange-soaked hills.

Good morning! We glow at dawn.

Hello, early light!

Hello, slush and snow.

Hello. In the sunlight, I soak into the cold ground.
In the shadow, I stay still and icy.

Hello, winter thaw.

Hello, new leaves.

Hello, waking animals!

Hello, bright sun!

I warm the land!

Hello, budding flowers.
Hello, bright-blue pond.
Hello, running brook.
Hello, green grass all, all over.
Hello, robins!

Hello! Our petals blossom.
The fish are awake.
Streams run down the hills.
Morning dew is on the meadows.
The birds have come back!

Goodbye, winter.

Hello, spring!

To James, Martha, and Chris

Henry Holt and Company, *Publishers since 1866*
Henry Holt® is a registered trademark of Macmillan Publishing Group, LLC
120 Broadway, New York, NY 10271
mackids.com

Library of Congress Cataloging-in-Publication Data is available.
ISBN 978-1-250-15172-8

Our books may be purchased in bulk for promotional, educational, or business use. Please contact your local bookseller or the
Macmillan Corporate and Premium Sales Department at (800) 221-7945 ext. 5442 or by email at MacmillanSpecialMarkets@macmillan.com.

First edition, 2020
Designed by Kenard Pak and Mallory Grigg
The artist used watercolor and pencil, digitally enhanced, to create the illustrations for this book.
Printed in China by RR Donnelley Asia Printing Solutions Ltd., Dongguan City, Guangdong Province

5 7 9 10 8 6 4